Charlotte's Web™

Coloring and Activity Book and Stamps

By Julia Simon-Kerr

Illustrated by Boyd Kirkland

Based on the Motion Picture Screenplay
by Susanna Grant and Karey Kirkpatrick

Based on the book by E. B. White

HarperEntertainment
An Imprint of HarperCollinsPublishers

SPRING IS IN THE AIR

TIME FOR SCHOOL

Fern is going to school, and Wilbur wants to go with her.
Help him get through the maze to find her.

START

FINISH

Answer key on page 32.

FERN'S SECRET

Shhhhhh! Fern has a secret!
Fill in the vowels in the words below to find out what it is.

W_LB_R   _S   H_D_NG

_N   H_R   D_SK

Answer key on page 32.

PIG'S OUT!

FUN IN THE MUD

The best thing about springtime rain is mud!

FLOWER TIME

You'll need a friend to play this game. Each player takes turns connecting the flowers, one at a time, to make a square. When you complete a square, put your stamp in it. You can use your opponent's lines to make a square. The player with the most squares wins!

THE NAME GAME

When Wilbur moves to the barn, he has to learn everyone's name.
Figure out the names of each animal by using the code below.

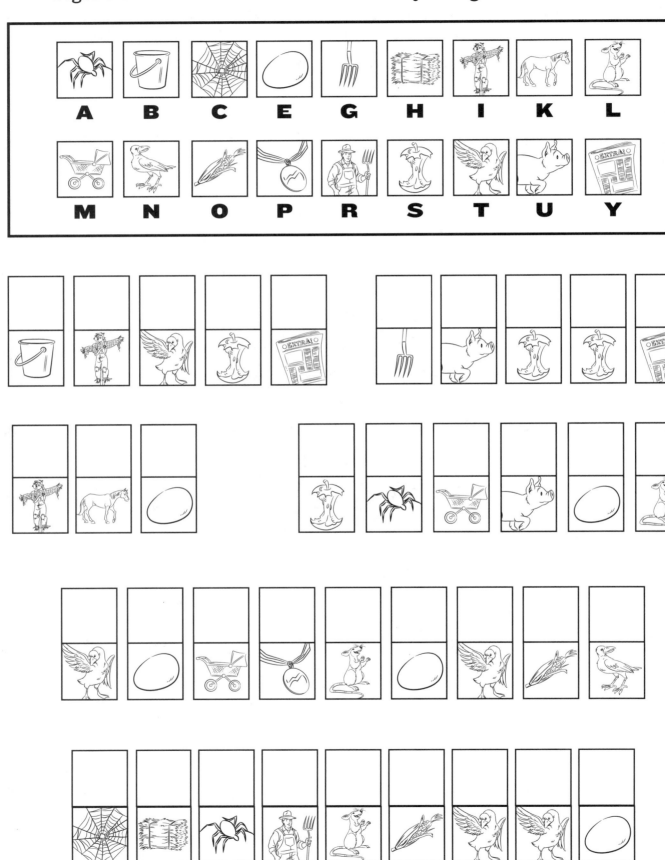

EGG ROLL

Help Templeton get Gussy's egg into his underground lair
without crossing underneath another tunnel.

START

FINISH

Answer key on page 32.

SUMMER TURNS TO FALL

Everything is changing on Zuckerman's farm.

TOPSY-TURVY

Things are topsy-turvy in the barn, and not just because Avery is trying to trap Charlotte. Find at least eleven things wrong in this scene.

THE PROMISE

Charlotte works on saving Wilbur before winter.

FIXIN' FEATHERS

Gussy the goose is fixing her feathers in the barn. Can you help her?
Study the pictures below and circle the picture that is not like the others.

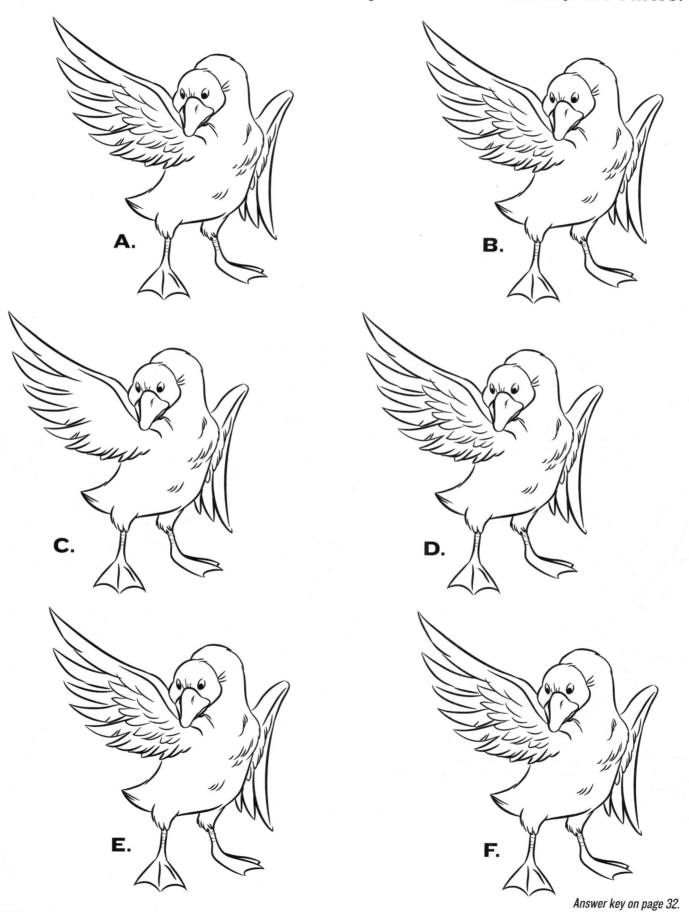

Answer key on page 32.

AT THE DUMP

Templeton visits one of his favorite places.
He is looking for words for Charlotte.

A FRIENDLY NEIGH-BOR

Use the grid below as a guide to draw your own picture of Ike.

PLANTING AN IDEA

Fern thinks a flyer about the County Fair might give Mr. Zuckerman the right idea about Wilbur.

FUN WITH FRIENDS

You'll need a friend to play this game. Each player should pick a stamp. Using the grids below, play your very own Charlotte's Web version of tic-tac-toe.

PAINTED CROWS

Templeton knows how to get the pesky crows off his back!

WORD WIZ

Can you find all the words related to Zuckerman's farm?
The words are hidden reading forward, backward,
up, down, or diagonally in either direction.

```
O Q Z E C E D L F H P Z
S A L U T A T I O N S C
T I U S F H P J R C Z R
F E U P U V X E E C A Y
Q F M M M H F Y Q H T A
X H B P K Q U V M A P O
S L P B L I K E O R Z S
E P S M R E P M F L Y R
K V O E C D T X P O L D
N I L L E T Y O G T L I
U R S C S L G S N T O H
R U B L I W L L Q E G J
```

CHARLOTTE	SALUTATIONS
FERN	SLOPS
GOLLY	TEMPLETON
HUMBLE	WILBUR
IKE	

Answer key on page 32.

CHARLOTTE'S WEB

Charlotte is spinning another word for Wilbur.
Connect the dots to find out what it is.

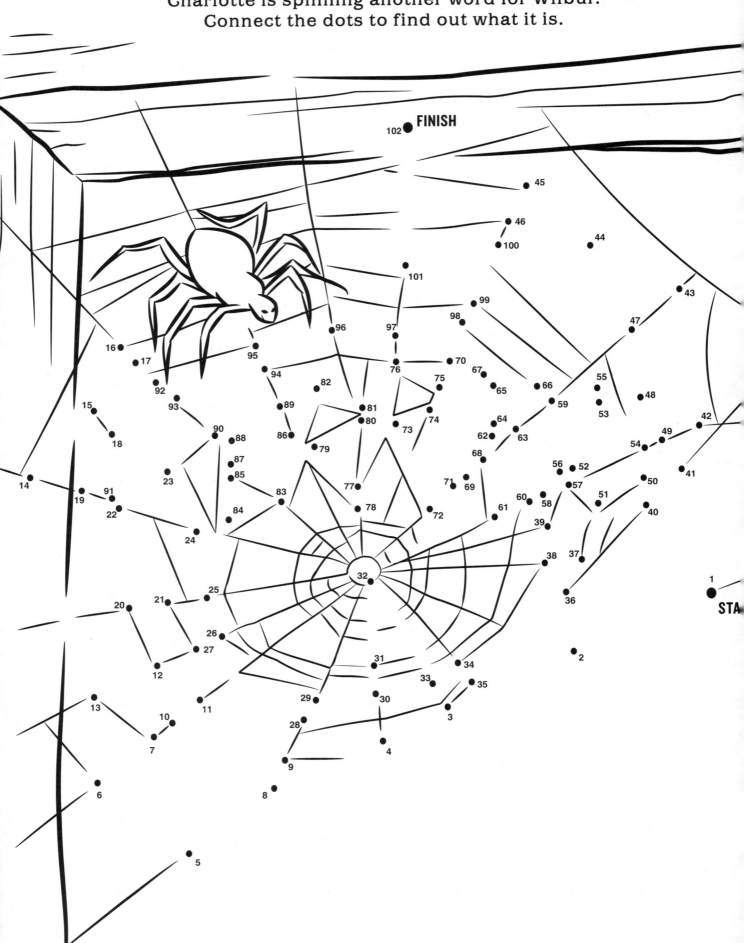

STAYING OUT OF THE SPOTLIGHT

Charlotte and Templeton want to stay out of the spotlight at the County Fair. Find Wilbur's two friends hidden in Wilbur's stall.

Answer key on page 32.

TOUGH COMPETITION

Wilbur's next-door neighbor may not be the smartest
pig in the pen, but he sure is big!

SOME PIG

Wilbur is the most radiant, terrific, humble pig at the fair!

A SPECIAL FRIEND

Wilbur would not have won his medal without the help of one special friend.
Follow the directions below and you'll always end up pointing to her.

1. Point to any web.
2. Move your finger left or right to the nearest medal, even if you have to skip boxes.
3. Move your finger up or down to the nearest web. It may be up to three boxes away.
4. Move diagonally to the nearest medal.
5. Move up or left to find the special friend.

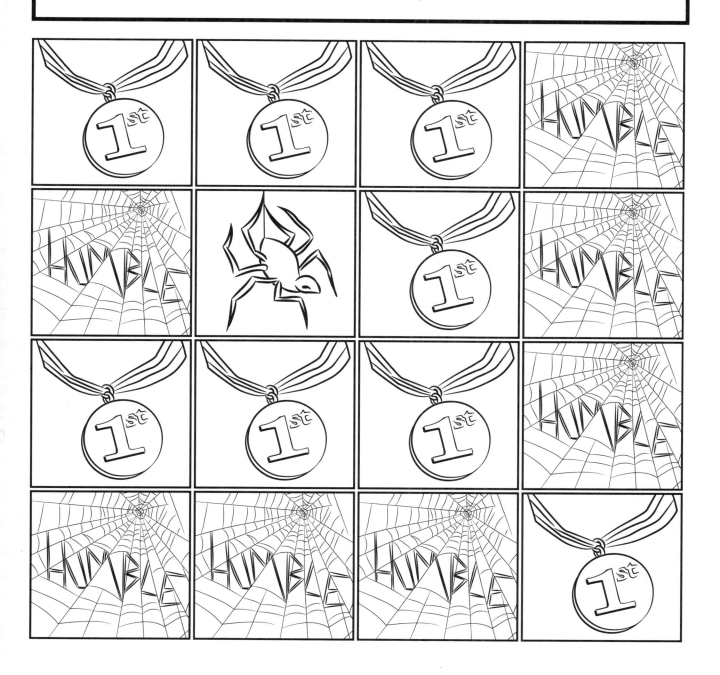

ANOTHER MIRACLE

Because of one very special spider,
Wilbur sees the most amazing sight—snow!

SALUTATIONS

Finally! The day Wilbur has been
waiting for has arrived.

ANSWER KEY

TIME FOR SCHOOL:

FERN'S SECRET:

WILBUR IS HIDING IN HER DESK

THE NAME GAME:

Bitsy, Gussy, Ike, Samuel, Templeton, and Charlotte

EGG ROLL:

TOPSY-TURVY:

1) Avery is wearing two different kinds of shoes.
2) Fern is sitting on Samuel the sheep.
3) One of the fences of the barnyard looks like a castle wall.
4) There is a palm tree in the scene.
5) A baby goose is wearing glasses.
6) Templeton is almost as big as Wilbur.
7) Wilbur is wearing sunglasses.
8) Samuel the sheep has a flower pot on his head.
9) There's an open laptop on a bale of hay.
10) Bitsy the cow is wearing slippers.
11) Mr. Arable is walking on his hands

FIXIN' FEATHERS: C

WORD WIZ:

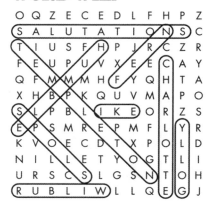

STAYING OUT OF THE SPOTLIGHT: